T0164642

THE MYSTIC MUSEUM

By
Raydin Ali

Order this book online at www.trafford.com
or email orders@trafford.com

Most Trafford titles are also available at major online book retailers.

© Copyright 2010 Raydin Ali.
All rights reserved. No part of this publication may be reproduced, stored
in a retrieval system, or transmitted, in any form or by any means, electronic,
mechanical, photocopying, recording, or otherwise, without
the written prior permission of the author.

Printed in Victoria, BC, Canada.

ISBN: 978-1-4269-1138-5 (sc)

*Our mission is to efficiently provide the world's finest, most
comprehensive book publishing service, enabling every author to
experience success. To find out how to publish your book, your way, and
have it available worldwide, visit us online at www.trafford.com*

Trafford rev. 10/06/2010

 www.trafford.com

North America & international
toll-free: 1 888 232 4444 (USA & Canada)
phone: 250 383 6864 ♦ fax: 812 355 4082

TABLE OF CONTENTS

ACKNOWLEDGEMENT

I, Raydin, would like to thank first my Mom, for typing my story. Also I wish to acknowledge the help I received from my Brother, Griffin. My Brother helped to interject a few ideas that have assisted me in clarifying some parts of this mystery story. I would like to thank my Grandma for helping with proof reading my story, inserting periods and capital letters were they were needed. Last of all I would like to thank my Dad for all his hard work preparing my story, the pictures, cover page and everything in order to get it published.

FORWARD

MY NAME IS Raydin, and I began to write my story when I was twelve years old and in grade seven. I wanted to have my story published as a novel as soon as possible.

The idea of writing a book came to me when I was just nine years old, Of course, it took me some time to decide just what kind of story I wanted to write.

My Grandma had written a book and dedicated it to my Brother, myself and my cousins. I was happy to see my name in print and on a book. I guess this is were I got the idea to write my own novel.

Then my twin Brother, Griffin, wrote an adventure story, which is now published. It is called, The Adventures of Diamond Guy. So I decided to write a story that sounded mysterious and called it, The Mystic Museum.

As I grow older, I would write more stories and publish them for everyone to read and to be proud of me. So look out for more of my stories.

DEDICATION

I DEDICATE THIS book to my twin Brother, Griffin and my wonderful pet dog, Angel who helps to look after me.

INTRODUCTION

EVERYBODY LOVES ADVENTURES, whether they are real or read from a book. So do I. At thirteen years old, I still dream that one day I would have a real adventure. Of course this was a dream which I never thought would come true. So boys and girls, and all of you out there, be careful what you dream about. You may be more than surprised when your dream comes true, or when you do have a real adventure.

Now bear with me while I tell you of my very weird but real life adventure. It was one that held so much mystery, so I call it my mysterious adventure, or maybe it was a dream that seems too real to be a dream. Yet these revelations still live with me today and have opened my eyes to a reality that I never knew existed.

So now I try to live a normal life, enjoy living with my friends and doing what most eleven year old boys do. I enjoy sports very much. I play hockey like my Mom and Auntie T, and I even go to their games to cheer them on.

My Dad likes soccer and plays with his teams. I go to watch him sometimes. He plays really well and I cheer his team on also. I think most people play sports especially when they are young and enjoy it. But as they grow older they find other things they like more, and do the things they like best. But I like hockey and will be playing it for a long time.

CHAPTER ONE:
POSSIBLE TO IMPOSSIBLE

"Raydin, Raydin, you're flying,"yelled my twin Brother, Griffin. Wow, that's so impossible as I am an ordinary little boy. How did this happen? Sometimes adventures happen to people when they least expect it. Yet, when it does happen, it leaves a lasting impression on one's memory and completely changes their outlook on life.

I know that whatever happens, we have to always turn it into something good. Something that will be of use to others, not something that will destroy or torment our society, but something that will be helpful to all. Goodness always pays off in the end, and I know that you reap what you sow, so I try always to be good and to do good things.

All children love to have fun and enjoy their young lives. They love to go out and experience as many things as they can for the sake of enjoyment. I am no different. I was a normal little boy eager to have my share of fun before I had to grow up and enter the adult jungle of work and family cares. But now my life has changed. I don't know if it is for the better or worse, only time will tell. I stay positive and keep on doing good things as my parents taught me to do.

This was my story, as I, Raydin, innocently went with my Dad and my twin Brother, Griffin to the Mystic Museum that lay somewhere in Saskatchewan. It is a very difficult thing to find because it is not greatly advertised and lies hidden in an out of the way deserted area, surrounded by mountains.

At one time, that area called Boca, was a thriving little farm town. People loved it as it was sheltered by the mountains. Now most of its settlers have either died or have moved away. You could still see traces of old farm houses and barns and a few people still live there. They plant crops and still rear a few cows, horses and the odd goat.

CHAPTER TWO:
MONSTERS FROM THE PAST

MY BROTHER AND I like to study old history. We became hooked on it when we visited the Dinosaur Museum in Drumheller. It is a northern town in Alberta, where a lot of dinosaur bones have been found. Some archeologists tried to piece the bones together and came up with these very large animals from long ago. Now they have turned the area into a large museum site. Here lots of people visit regularly to view these ancient monstrous animals.

Some were as long as a football playing field, and as high as a two story house. Their eggs were

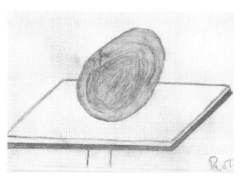 about two feet in height, about thirty inches wide and were elongated in shape. I had never seen such a large

egg before. I told my Dad that it could just about feed all the kids in my class for breakfast.

After looking at more of those huge dinosaurs, I thought that they may have been terrifying to any humans that lived at that time. Boy, was I glad that I was not living with them. I would really have been afraid of them. Maybe I would hide somewhere and not get a chance to play and have fun like I do now.

Our visit to this Dinosaur museum took us about two to three hours. After looking at the exhibits, we had lunch at the restaurant there. As usual, I had Hawaiian pizza which I love. My Brother and Dad both had a hamburger with onion rings. We talked about which exhibit was most intriguing. I liked the Pterodactyl and my Brother liked the Megladon. My Dad then took us back to get pictures of us near the Dinosaurs of our choice. We were happy to do so. I looked so tiny next to the Pterodactyl. My Brother also looked like an ant beside the Megladon.

When we came out of the museum, we took pictures of the model dinosaur that had greeted us outside of the museum. It was fun to stand beside them and even touch them. Other kids there were very excited to see them also. We really enjoyed our visit after we looked at these ancient animals. We were glad to have visited but we had to go, so we left to go home. Our day at the museum was quite exciting.

Now we had pictures of these tremendous creatures as souvenirs and memories. We planned to add them to our souvenir pictures of Mexico, where we had been visiting the year before. I just hope our album has space for these new pictures because we took a load of pictures of the exhibits. My Dad took some pictures and my Brother and I took our own with our cameras.

Dad was going to buy us souvenir T-shirts. My Brother chose one that had several pictures of dinosaurs. I chose one with a T Rex on the front. I knew he was a meat eater. Dinosaurs had fascinated me even before I went to kindergarten. I even had a large one given to me as a birthday gift. It sure looked real to me and has become one of my treasures. I'll try to keep it forever.

CHAPTER THREE:
OUR NEXT DECISION

O N OUR WAY home from the Dinosaur Museum, we talked our Dad into taking us to the really old, kind of forgotten Mystic Museum which was in an out of the way part of Saskatchewan. He agreed, then he said that he would have to look at a map to find out just where it was located. He planned to look at his map that he kept at home. So we drove on until we got home.

Then Dad made us a delicious supper of spaghetti and meat sauce. We ate ravenously, then showered and went to bed as Dad had told us to do. We soon fell into dreamland. I got up sweating. I had a nightmare. A big T Rex was chasing after me to make me his supper. My Grandma had once told me that we dream whatever we saw or thought during that day. Dad told me to turn over my pillow and go back to sleep. I did and my dreams surely changed. Now it was a more pleasant dream about my sports. When I woke up I was in a happy mood.

We knew that our Dad seemed to love adventure and was caught up in our enthusiasm to see this old museum. He had never ever been to one so old. So as soon as we went to bed, he took out his map and checked for this old museum. Finally he found its location. Then he went on to plot the shortest route to get there. When he was satisfied with his directions, he too went to bed.

I woke up again asking

"Dad is it time to get up?".

He told me that I had many more hours to sleep as it was only 10 pm. I could not seem to fall asleep. The excitement was too much for me. So I stayed awake for a long time before the sandman closed my eyes. My last waking thoughts were about my finding treasure, or looking at some long forgotten priceless piece of jewelry. This time I had much better dreams. I dream't that I was digging a hole to plant a tree in our backyard. Then I hit something hard that turned into a box of old treasure. Then I woke up to realize that it was only a dream.

CHAPTER FOUR: JOURNEY TO THE UNKNOWN

THE NEXT MORNING, we arose early, ate our breakfast of hash browns potatoes, sausages, and of course fruit juice. Then we packed drinks, snacks and a few sandwiches. We also added some fresh fruit. Yes, we are growing boys and needed a lot of food. So when we were all packed, which was about 9 am, we took off for this museum. We knew that we had at least a three hour drive to get there.

Needless to say, I was still pretty tired since I had little sleep the night before. So it is no wonder that I fell fast asleep in the car. Griffin soon followed me. We woke up because Dad had to drive around a really steep corner, and Griffin fell over on me. We stayed awake for the rest of the way.

The road was really rough. It had lots of potholes as if it was really neglected. We were now driving into an area that was completely surrounded by mountains. There seemed to be few houses around, at least in the area we were now passing. There were so many trees. It looked as if the forest was taking over the land. I was a bit fearful to be going into a kind of jungle, but tried to stay calm.

Here and there we could see traces of old broken down farm house and barns. There were also a few farm houses where people still lived. We also saw the odd horse or cow and a small school. I counted only three dogs. Two were just sitting and one was jumping around with two children. They stopped to watch us go by and I waved at them

CHAPTER FIVE:
THE MYSTIC MUSEUM

AT LAST WE spotted the Mystic Museum. It was brightly lit up. The bright lights helped to cheer me up. Now I was anxious to go in and see if there was any treasure inside. So I quickly jumped out of the car. I noticed that the old car parking lot was full of cracks in the cement. Also, it looked mildewed with moss covering many of its parts. There were two other cars parked outside. So we walked into the museum. It was not a very large building. There was the main structure, which was the middle part, and then there were two very large wings built on both sides. At the back, there was also a very large expansion. All together, I would say that it was almost as big as a football field, and had only one level. The entire building was constructed of stone bricks and was well kept. It housed quite a few exhibits. Some were really very old so they were like treasures.

Its walls were repainted sometime ago, and the paint had now begun to fade. There were no cobwebs on the walls. I noticed that right away because I am afraid of spiders. We noticed that there were a number of flowers in large pots, both on the outside of the museum and in the inner foyer. They sure brightened up the place.

Someone mentioned that the flowers were marigolds and daisy. I assumed that the yellows ones were the marigolds and the pink ones were the daisies. Whatever they were they were beautiful.

There was a large area around the museum that had been cleared of trees, and allowed for three picnic areas. This made the place seem rather friendly and warm. So, anyone could picnic at the sides or at the back. There were a few picnic tables and some play structures for small children. We were told about these by the guy who was working outside of the Museum. He looked like he was keeping the picnic area clean.

I preferred to stay indoors and look around. It was more fun for me. I was looking eagerly for my expected treasure, and I know that it could only be found inside the museum.

CHAPTER SIX:
THINGS OF INTEREST

A S WE LEFT the foyer and stepped inside, we met the curator. He was a middle aged man who wore his glasses on his nose. We were charged a reasonable fee. He explained that it was just enough to cover the cost of up keeping the museum. The light bill, he said is the most expensive. Then the museum was cleaned once a month and the grounds had to be upkept. So we did not mind paying.

Besides, I was most anxious to look for my treasure.

Right away we found out that we were not there before anyone else, others had come and left already. So the curator took us to look at some native artifacts. He seemed proud of the artifacts because he was a half descendant of the tribe that lived there long ago about eighty years. The tribal people had settled there. Some had intermarried with the new settlers, but most of the older people had died and others had moved away. The curator himself looked like he was around forty years old and but still lived close by.

There were numerous arrow heads and spears. Some beautiful beaded clothing was on display, together with roughly made Ticanagans and snow shoes. The women carried their babies in these Ticanagans on their backs. There were also a few dream catchers of different sizes they were all very beautiful. The entire Tribe used snowshoes to get around during the winter months. There were also birch bark canoes and pictures of dog sleds. In all I think that these tribal people thought of their harsh environment and found clever or ingenious ways to overcome all of their obstacles.

He did show us a tepee which I though was a real practical house, because they could be easy to transport. They were comfortable and made of animal hide. There was also a peace pipe used in religious ceremonies. We also saw stuffed animals that were used for food or for transport. I admired their idea of taking only what they need from nature and trying to use all of it so there would be no pollution. They looked like a remarkable people.

CHAPTER SEVEN:
OUR CHOICE OF DISPLAYS

O<small>UR GUIDE THEN</small> left us to attend to other visitors who were just arriving at the museum. I noticed that there were about three or four other parties. So we wondered around and browsed at the religious section of the first foreign settlers that moved to Canada. There were a display of china, pots and pans, tools, furniture and clothing. These did not peak my interest so I joined my Brother and wandered around to the Egyptian artifacts.

Since we had already studied some parts of the Egyptian Pharaohs as well as their Pyramids and Sphinxes, it was really easy for us to appreciate and understand the artifacts. Looking at real life artifacts though, was very different than reading about them and looking at the pictures. The real thing was indeed startling. Some were miniature artifacts but they look real to us.

We were able to see some of the actual objects, and actually touch them; which we did when we thought that no one was looking. It felt magical to my touch. We knew that we were not supposed to touch anything, but being young boys, we just couldn't help it.

I kept staring at the large copy of the Pyramid and the Sphinx. They mystified me so much that I stood motionless for a long time. I thought about the labour that went to make these and wondered just what purpose they served. No one would build enormous monuments for no reason. Now after about three thousand years we still don't know why they were built.

The replica of the Tut-en-camon, the boy king did not hold much of my interest. I found the mummies to be kind of scary so I skipped them. Yet Griffin's eyes were glued to them. He was quite fascinated by them. I was looking at the other replicas of artifact. Their armour and helmets were beautiful, and glittered like gold.

Chariots were used in those days and the one on display was a magnificent replica. The Egyptians were very clever people. They even had their own writing system. It was an amazing one, although I could not read any of it. I thought of becoming an archeologist to understand the past and who can decipher ancient manuscripts and be like those who can read hieroglyphics. I wonder if their jobs were fun.

CHAPTER EIGHT:
WE HAD TO TOUCH

GRIFFIN STUCK HIS hand into the King's throne enclosure to touch it. He thought that it was real gold. So my Dad told him to keep his hands away from the exhibits because the sign said "Do not touch".

Also there were other people walking around to look at the exhibits. Mom and Dad did not want us to ever do anything wrong. They always taught us to do the right thing but enjoy ourselves, and we listen to them.

Then we moved to the wax exhibits. They sure looked like people who were really alive and not wax people. I did not know the people whom they represented. I could only tell the one that was the Queen of England and Elvis Presley, but no more. I was really amazed at that type of Art and wondered just how it was done.

Next was the war exhibits. Some of them were pretty scary. I began to think of how foolish a war was. We were all here on earth to help and protect each other, not to kill one another. Boy, I vowed never to become a soldier or even participate in any wars. They are a horrendous waste of life.

The next exhibit was the stuffed animals and birds that had lived long ago on the Prairies. There were the deer, the moose, the caribou and others which I immediately recognized. The male deer had such large antlers, and so did the moose and caribou. It was amazing to see.

Then I looked at the snowy owl. It was remarkable to see. It looked so real, and I even really liked it. We soon heard the announcement that the museum was going to close in five minutes. Dad motioned for us to head out, but you know how little boys are. We just had to linger as long as possible. I had to touch the snowy owl to know how soft its feathers were.

CHAPTER NINE:
END OF OUR VISIT

W E SAW THAT everyone was heading for the front doors. When Dad told us to
"get a move on,"
we still tried to put our hands on the deer to feel its fur. Then as we headed for the front door, Griffin blurted out
"I have to go back to the Egyptian display,"
Dad said,
"we have no time for that."
Then Griffin said
"I left my wallet on the wall next to the mummies in the Egyptian section."
So we knew we had to go back. Of course, Dad was mad at him, but Dad never yelled at us boys. He just remarked that Griffin should not be so careless in the future. Then he took our hands and tried to hurry us back to the Egyptian section to get the wallet that Griffin had forgotten. He wanted us to hurry so we could get out of the doors before they were shut.

As soon as we got to the display, which was way at the back of the museum, Griffin found his wallet which he had left and grabbed it. We then turned around to head back to the front doors. As we made a few steps, the lights in the museum was shut off and we heard the doors bang shut.

Dad yelled just then. He said

"Hey, do not lock us in. We are almost out. We are still in here. Let us out. Do not leave us in here."

But no one answered back. The museum of course was quite dark. Dad made us hold his hands. He said,

"I do not want to loose you boys so hold on and stay close to me."

So we did what he said and we held his hands and followed him closely.

CHAPTER TEN:
LOCKED IN

IT TOOK US a while for our eyes to adjust to the darkness but we did and got to the front doors. Right away we started pounding on them as loudly as we could, with the hope that someone would hear us. After a long while, we gave up and Dad told us to hold hands to make sure that we stay together and not lose one another. He mentioned that he had seen a door on the side of the museum, and we gripped his hands as we headed there.

Luckily Dad had a small light on his key ring. So he used it to help us find our way to this back door. He kept on saying

"Keep holding hands. Do not let go. I do not want to lose anyone of you."

So we listened and kept on holding hands and following Dad as he tried to find that door. I wondered if we could open it at all because the locks were so rusted.

At last he found the door. It was on an old stone wall with an old metal door. The door had bolted locks on it. There were bolted locks in the middle of the door and bolts at the top and bottom. You could tell that this door was never used for a long time because it was quite rusted.

Now Dad asked us to hold the lights and flash it at the locks so he could try to open them. There was a chain attached to the top lock, and he got it open with a bit of trouble. The bolt at the middle also got opened with a lot of turning and twisting because of the rust. Then came the bolt at the bottom of the door. It gave a lot of trouble, but Dad is strong and with a lot of twisting and pulling, it finally gave way and opened.

Well, we were all very happy that we were out of the museum. Now, all we had to do was walk around and find the parking lot where we had left our car, and head for home. By this time, it was already getting dark and we were not sure how to find the parking lot. Dad told us to stick together and follow him. Then he put both his hands out and each of us took a hand and held on tightly.

CHAPTER ELEVEN: OUR JOY

NOW WE WERE out of the museum and had to try to find our way to the car park to find our car. Dad's idea was to stay close to the building, because there were bushes and tall trees not far from the museum. He told us to stay on the cement foot path that we knew went all around the museum. We also hoped that there were no wild animals in those bushes that may cause us harm. So we kept on walking slowly feeling our way along as there was no light to guide us.

I was in front of Dad, and my Brother was behind Dad. Oh yes! I listened to my Dad and was walking slowly, trying to get my eyes accustomed to the outside. I was kind of feeling my way around because the ground was high and low, not smooth like a new path. I was remembering what Dad said,

"Take your time, easy does it. We're doing fine."

On my next step, I felt like there was a rock under my foot. Then before I could say

"Look out,"

to Griffin and Dad, the whole slab of rock moved downwards like a trap door. The three of us slid down underground into some sort of cave or something. Dad's voice rang out,

"boys don't panic, just stick together and stay cool. Are you boys O.K.?"

We both answered together,

"Yes, Dad."

We used the light to see if there was an opening, and to find a way to climb back out, but there was none. There were only smooth rocks around us. We had, no way to get out, because there was no stairs or rock formations that we could climb on to get to the top. We saw nothing that could help us. We had fallen on some sort of sandy bed which was the bottom of the cave, so we were not injured. I was thankful that I had no broken bones or else I would have been in a lot of pain.

Our idea was to get to the top and try to tilt the slab that we had fallen through; but we found no way. We felt trapped and we were really trapped. I was getting terrified now, and began to cry, but Dad hugged me and told me that we would be alright. He asked us to be brave, and we felt better.

CHAPTER TWELVE:
STRANGE BEINGS

W̶E FOUND OURSELVES trapped in this cave. Even if one of us stood on Dad's shoulder, which we tried, we could not reach the top. Dad knew that even if we did reach the top, neither Griffin nor I had the strength to push up the heavy cement slab. So that idea was now scrapped. We had to find some other way to get out.

My heart started to pound with fear, and I began to cry. Dad soothed me by saying that it was all right, he was with us and would protect us. Then he told us to try to get some sleep while he tried to figure a way out. But we could not fall asleep. We were still somewhat scared. Then Dad gave up, because he was tired too. He put us on both sides of him, then he bundled us in his arms to still our fears. I was on one arm and my Brother was on the other arm. As we felt secured now, we fell asleep.

I don't know for how long we slept, but I awoke with a jolt, because I felt that both my legs and arms were being held and I was being carried.

My first thought was that I was being rescued. So I opened my eyes and I saw two human like glowing creatures holding me and taking me into a tunnel. I thought I was dreaming, so I tried to turn over, but soon realized that I was not dreaming. This was real! I was scared!

I looked for my Dad and Brother but I could not see them. Then I tried to yell, but no sound came out of my mouth. So I lifted my head as much as I could to see who those creatures were. A soft glow brightened up the cave. I noticed that the walls were carved out of the rocks. I kept my head up to try to find any clue as to where I was, but I found none at all.

These creatures had a kind of scaly plated skin. They had arms with wrist and elbows like ours, but their arms were also covered with the same scaly plate skin as was their entire bodies. The plates on their head was a bit larger than those on their bodies, and helped to emit the glowing light that I had seen when I first opened my eyes. They had slits for eyes and mouth but no ears, and somehow they seemed friendly and caring. They handled me very gently.

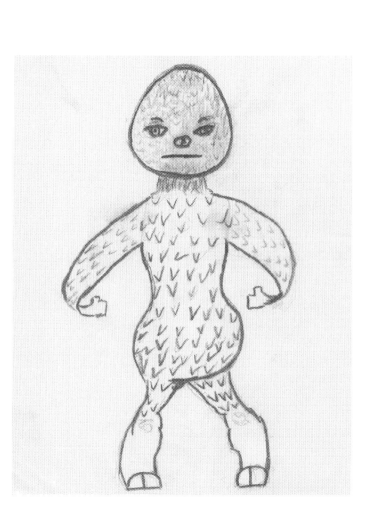

CHAPTER THIRTEEN:
A BIT OF REVELATION

A FTER A LITTLE while, I noticed that the narrow cave ended in a large sort of room. Here they put me down. The room was lighted and warm, but there was no fire or flames of any kind. I saw crude trays hollowed out of rocks filled with fruit. They motioned for me to eat with some crude hand gestures. I was scared of them. I wondered if they were going to hurt me. So I started to cry. They began to move away from me to kind of reassure me that they would not harm me.

Then I asked for my Dad and Brother; but they did not speak to me. I looked again at them and realized that the slits I thought were mouths, were just a thin strip of bone. They really had no mouths. They seem to be trying to calm me with their minds, but their language was different to ours. Then I felt that I knew their language and I became calm. I knew they were not going to hurt me.

They left me in the room and as I looked around, I saw that there were spikes on one of the walls. These spikes were not parallel to each other, but the spikes on the left were kind of in between those on the right. I wondered what these wooden looking spikes were for. I noticed that they were perfectly made.

I did not have much time to think because I saw that these glowing creatures were heading back into this room. They arrived bringing my Brother and Dad the same way they had brought me. Then they placed Dad and Griffin beside me and motioned for us to eat. Boy, was I glad to see my Dad and Brother. I felt much better now.

The creatures telepathically told me that they had long awaited me, Raydin, the master of their kingdom. They said that they were not trying to hurt us, but wanted us to eat and rest in the warm room and they would see us after we had rested. Then they left. I told my Dad what they had said as he couldn't understand their language. He wasn't sure if I was just making it up, but I told him that I understood their language. I just don't know if they believed me.

CHAPTER FOURTEEN:
OUR DISCOVERY

D AD TRIED THE berries, and told us we could eat them. He said that they tasted like ordinary earth berries. So we both ate a few as we had no supper that day. The blue berries and cranberries were quite juicy, so we did not need a drink.

Griffin got up and walked over to the wall and leaned on one spike and shifted around a bit. Then he put a foot on the spike opposite to the one he was leaning on. His actions triggered a flap on the opposite wall. It was a door. We saw that it led to another cave, but the flap was high up on the wall and we couldn't get through.

Then Griffin tried two more spikes and they opened a larger flap. Since there were six spikes in all we tried them all and found that they opened another door on the opposite side of the cave. The last set of spikes opened a fairly large door on that same wall. We could see that each door led to a tunnel. There were three tunnels in all.

So we took the one on the left. It lead us to a large room that was partially lighted. Dad motioned us to be really quiet. We noticed that there was more than one cave there. As we got closer, we saw that it was like the home of the creatures, for there were many of them asleep in the caves.

As we did not want to wake them up, we went back through the tunnel to the cave where they had first taken us. Then we tried the middle tunnel. It led us to another large cave that had a huge hollow in the middle. We saw what looked like a metal object oblong in shape and what looked like mummified set of the creatures. So we quickly turned back into the tunnel and went back to the room with the food where the creatures had first taken us.

Then we had just one last tunnel to explore to see if it would lead us out of the caves. So we went into the last tunnel with a prayer on in our hearts. We desperately wanted to get out of these caves and go home. We were quite tired and I thought how good my bed would feel if I could be on it just then.

CHAPTER FIFTEEN:
OUR LUCK IS GOOD

THE TUNNEL ON the right was the last one to explore, so we headed there. We ended up with a wall instead of a cave. I was so disappointed. Dad flashed his light up and down the cave. In doing that, Griffin saw a bunch of squares near to the bottom of the wall. There was also a bunch of weird writing which we could not figure out. We though it might be some kind of instructions.

Then Griffin began to trace some of the weird writing with his finger. He soon made what looked like a crown face. While showing it to us he hit it with his hand. We saw a flap. Then Griffin discovered that there was a line of crown faces and he began punching them. It opened a space large enough for one of the creatures to get through. We soon realized that it was a short passage that led us back to the sandy bed where we had first fallen so we went there.

Dad looked around with his light and saw we were right back in the cave where we first fell. So he told us boys to try to get some sleep and he would stay awake to guard us. I crouched down right by Dad's foot and was tired. So I yawned and said

"goodnight "

to my Brother.

As usual Griffin kept changing spots in the cave. He was trying to get a comfortable spot. Then when he got to one spot he lay down and got up fast. He began to dig the sand. Dad asked him just what he was doing. He said

"I felt something hard like a rock when I went to lie down so I am trying to remove it and get comfortable."

This woke me from my half sleep state. Dad flashed the light for him to see what he was doing.

To Griffin's surprise, he found a sort of handle, so he pulled on it with all of his might. Then, surprise! It opened the trap door on the top. It was the very one that we fell through. Now we could see that the dawn was clearing. The place was not so bright as yet. Dad told us to sleep until he could figure out a way to get out.

CHAPTER SIXTEEN:
OUT, OUT, OUT

A s THE DAYLIGHT brightened above us, Dad realized that the opening was too high for us to reach. Also it was still a bit dark outside. Later on he kind of snoozed away too, as we were all tired from the sleepless night we had spent.

During my sleep, I was dreaming that the creatures had come back for us. So I yelled loudly in my dream. My yell woke me up and also woke up my Dad and Brother. They asked me what happened to make me yell. So I told them about my dream. By then the sun was coming up and we could see its brightness through the opening.

Meanwhile, up above the curator had arrived for work and he saw our car still in the parking lot. He waited for his two assistants who came shortly after. They were wondering why our car was there and we were not. So they called but got no reply. So they began to look around the museum. Then they heard my loud yell and came running in our direction.

They saw the trap door, and as they looked down, they saw us three on the sandy bottom of the cave. My yell had brought the help we needed. Soon the curator had placed a ladder down into the opening, and we climbed up one by one. Dad sent us up first to make sure that we would be safe. He was the last to come up.

Dad then explained to the curator how we were locked in and came through the back door. Then as we tried to get to the car, we had fallen into that opening. They saw how deep it was, and decided to fill it up so that there would be no more accidents. We did not mention the creatures because they may not even believe us.

Everyone was so relieved to have us back on the surface. We were also happy to be on what we thought was solid ground once more. So Dad thanked everyone and we got into our car and headed home. We all felt relieved to be safe, and happy, and to be heading for home.

CHAPTER SEVENTEEN: OH NO! NOT AGAIN

GRIFFIN AND I were so tired from our Night time ordeal, but we tried to stay awake to keep Dad company and not let him fall asleep at the wheel. We were praising Griffin for getting us out of the cave and away from the creatures. He was the inquisitive one who found all of the levers to open all of the doors.

Then, at last, the sandman overcame us boys and we cuddled up in the back seat and fell asleep. The last thing I heard Dad say was that if we were hungry there was food and drinks in the cooler. He himself had taken a sandwich and some iced tea.

Suddenly we felt a jerk as the car stopped. Dad called to us to say that we were home and should get to bed. He then took out the cooler and went indoors. I suppose he also had headed for his bed after the grueling night. Griffin turned over and crawled out of the car and went indoors calling to me to come. I answered rather sleepily that I was coming, but I turned over and slept for a while.

Then I awoke with a jerk. I heard a funny sound, but I was too tired to care. As I was in the process of turning over, my eyes glimpsed two lighted beings. They had followed us home and were taking me with them. I felt so weak that I could not even yell or put up a fight and I was scared.

Some how they speedily took me back to the cave. There they told me again that I was Raydin their leader and chief scientist. They had waited a long time for me to return and were not going to lose me again. They really needed me to help them.

I was amazed and said that I was only a little boy and could not be their leader. I did not know them. One of the creatures quickly reached for a small round glowing object and as he came up to me, the other one restrained him. At this time I was alone with them and scared out of my mind. I began to cry and wanted them to take me home.

The one closest to me, who had befriended me, told me that they had come from their kingdom from the planet Venus where I was their ruler. Then their craft developed some kind of engine trouble and they fell to earth. They fell in the trees near the museum. They radioed for help and I had said that I would come to their assistance. So they waited and waited and in the meanwhile had built the caves in which to hide. They said that I was the chosen one, chosen by the people of Venus to rule; as I had the most knowledge and power. I did not believe them. I told them that they were mistaken. I was just a little boy.

Finally, their sensors indicated to them that I was near and they brought me back to help them. I asked,

"what kind of help do you need?"

They said that I was the only trained one to fix the craft. I laughed and told them that they were quite mistaken. I was only a little boy and had just started school and knew no science. I demanded that they take me home. I was now shouting and showing my anger and I saw that they had moved away a short distance from me. So I felt good.

CHAPTER EIGHTEEN:
THE CRAFT

WHEN I SAW their reaction, I felt that I had them scared so I had the upper hand. Man, was I wrong. Both of them came up to me and put that round glowing thing on my forehead. At first I felt paralyzed and thought I was going to die. I couldn't even speak. Suddenly I started to see visions slowly appearing like pictures.

The first one I saw was a huge person dressed in a metallic suit, with a special gold band stretched across his chest from his right shoulder to his left hip. I recognized him to be Raydin their leader and ruler. But he looked exactly like me! He was a very pleasant person and smiled a lot. Everyone liked him, and looked up to him. He was not only strong, but had some special powers. He could levitate and while floating in the air, fly at fast speed. From his hand he could shoot light or fire, and there were many other things that he could do.

These pictures showed the planet Venus. It was different to our Earth. They had no trees or flowers or animals like us, but the people were exactly like these creatures, covered with plates on their bodies. They were friendly and showed love to everyone. They were also very helpful and cooperated well. There were no wars or fighting or hatred. I also saw their advanced science and technology. Then they removed the glowing disc from my head.

It took me a while to settle down. Then I found that I could speak to them in their language. So I asked them what they needed. They told me that they needed help to repair their craft so they could get back to their home. Now I felt strong and powerful and let them lead me to their craft. They took me to cave number two where we had seen the metallic object.

That was the same one that we had seen the night before when we strayed into that cave and saw the mummies. So I went up to the craft and checked it out. Then I saw two burnt out bolts and a small hole in the power source. Somehow I knew how to fix it and I did. I used my powers and knowledge to rebuild the power source container and it worked. The engines fired up, they were glad to have their craft fixed and working.

Then they opened the rocks above the craft by pulling a lever on the wall. They tried the engine. At first it sputtered and coughed, but then it changed into a low whirling sound. Everyone around looked pleased. They raised their hands and shook them in the air; and then shook their heads at me in a nod as if to say well done.

At that point they began to reload their craft with the things they had brought. I did not realize that there were about twenty of them. So they boarded the craft. The last one came up to me and thanked me. He told me to close up the rock when the craft took off.

Then he handed me a shell that could fit in the palm of my hand. It looked kind of shiny, and could open and close. This was a communicating device, so they could communicate with me if there was need to do so I thanked them for it and wished them a good voyage home.

Before the craft took off, they took me through the opening into the trees where I stood. Then the craft ascended from the cave, made a small circular motion and lifted off noiselessly into the air and it was gone. It was gone in a matter of seconds. I tried to look at it until it disappeared. It moved away so fast that it literally disappeared from my view. I was amazed! I knew that no one would believe me

I stood there in shocked wonderment. Now I was all alone. My last job was to reseal the opening in the cave which I did. I pointed my hands at the spot and the dirt just collapsed back into place. It felt kind of lonely in the forest, and I remembered my Dad telling us that there might be unfriendly animals among the trees, so I quickly headed back towards the museum.

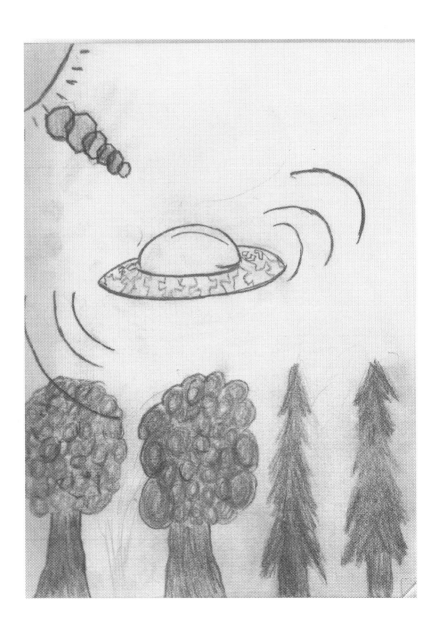

CHAPTER NINETEEN: DISBELIEF

Soon I found the clearing around the museum and came onto the same cement path we had walked on that morning. So I knew my way to the front of the museum. That was where I headed, I realized that it was late in the afternoon and suddenly I knew that my Dad and Brother may have missed me and were now searching for me.

So I hurried into the museum. The Curator was shocked to see me. He said that he thought we had gone home since early morning, and had no idea we were still here. Our car was gone. I then asked him to use his phone to call my Dad to come and get me. Now he thought that my Dad had forgotten me, so he let me use the phone.

My Dad answered the phone and was surprised to hear my voice on the other end. He asked

"Raydin, where are you? I though you were still asleep in your room?"

When I told him that I was at the museum, he could not believe me. He said

"Don't try any tricks on me son, I know I brought you home this morning."

It was hard to convince him where I was, but he knew we do not lie to him. So he said he would like to speak to the Curator. Dad knew that the museum would be closed in two hours, so he begged the Curator to stay with me until he got there. The Curator said that he would oblige, as I was only a little boy, which made me glad. I did not want to wait there alone, because I would be too scared.

The Curator asked if I was hungry. Although I said

"no",

he went to the vending machine and got me a sandwich and a drink. He kept me close to him all the time, and announced to the visitors that he was keeping the museum open an hour later than usual. So I stayed awake until my Dad arrived, when I saw him, I ran and threw my arms around him. Was I ever glad to see him and my Brother again.

On the way home I told them what had happened, they were amazed. They both assured me that the beings were gone now and would not kidnap me again. Dad was not so sure. He was nervous, thinking that they could just come back and get me whenever they wanted. Then I showed him the communication device and convinced him that they had indeed left. He was satisfied, and said

"I do not ever want to lose you son, I love you both too much."

CHAPTER TWENTY:
SECRET POWER

B Y THIS TIME I had fallen asleep in the car
again. When we got home, Dad made sure
that he took me out of the car, himself. When we
got inside, he sat on the couch holding me in his
arms and letting me sleep. He was not taking any
chances. He just kept us two boys with him all of
the time.

Two days later I had a hockey game. While
on the ice I felt that I could move with the speed
of light. Since I was unsure of this new kind of
power, I had to try real hard to show the team that
I was normal. I could not let anyone know about
my secret adventure and power. It was hard to
keep it under control, but I practiced hard. Sure
I used it to score twice and put our team in the
lead. After we won the game, I was glad to have
this power.

It happened a few days later when we went out
snowboarding. I sensed it before it happened, an
avalanche. I was able to get my Dad and Brother
to safety by making them follow me. Then the

whole wall of snow came tumbling down. We were safe but two other snowboarders who did not expect it, were trapped.

The avalanche was more than a half a kilometer wide. We stood looking at it and saw the two boys tumble and were then covered up by the snow. I knew they could not survive without help. So I felt the need to save them. Dad said he would phone for help, While he was doing that, I found that I could levitate and flew over the area where the boys were. That is when my Brother yelled at me

"Raydin you are flying".

Somehow I knew exactly where the boys were. Once I got over them I pointed my hand and melted most of the ice around them. Then I flew back to join Dad and Griffin. In a few minutes the boys easily dug themselves out of the snow and stood up. We were glad they were saved, and they did not know about my power. We called to them and told them that help was on the way.

Soon the rescue helicopters were spotted. They saw us three and noted that we were safe. Then they went and rescued the two boys. Everyone was happy that the boys did not perish. Again I was happy to have my new found power, and vowed to use it only for good reasons. I was always told to be a helpful person. My Dad and Brother hugged me and we headed for home. I knew I had to keep my power a secret from everyone else and I knew that there would be other times in my life when I would have to use it.

ABOUT THE AUTHOR

Raydin Ali is a soft spoken, brown haired, brown eyed, intelligent child, with beautiful olive skin. He enjoys learning about scientific discoveries, and likes to watch mysterious, comical and magical shows. Like all children, he enjoys reading adventure stories and those dealing with rags to riches.

Some of his hobbies are collecting cards, building things, working on jigsaw puzzles, drawing, swimming, and playing hockey. Hockey is his most loved sport and he plays on a team. He is a good player and an asset to his team.

While in grade three, he had a project which required drawing a picture so he drew an eagle in flight. His picture got the highest award.

Drawing is one of his hobbies. Most of the pictures in this book were done by him. They are his own composition. They were his own imagination and so was the story in this novel. Both story and pictures depict his active mind and vivid imagination. Like all children at his age their minds do focus on their own world and the glamour of it.

At least we know that his mind is pure and full of goodness. It is reflected in his story. So read about his mystery and enjoy the book.